MR. MAGORIUM'S WONDER EMPORIUM

Magical Movie Storybook

Adapted by Michael Anthony Steele
From the screenplay by Zach Helm

SCHOLASTIC INC.

New York   Toronto   London   Auckland   Sydney
Mexico City   New Delhi   Hong Kong   Buenos Aires

walden.com/magorium and **Magorium.com**

ISBN-13: 978-0-439-91252-5
ISBN-10: 0-439-91252-0

⬥ WALDEN MEDIA

12 11 10 9 8 7 6 5 4 3 2 1   7 8 9 10/0

Book design by Rick DeMonico and Heather Barber

Printed in China.
First printing, October 2007

Bellini the bookmaker peered through a magnifying glass as he worked. With the utmost care, he wrote tiny letters as he neared the end of a large yellow book. It was the last volume of a very long series.

The books contained a fantastic and wonderful tale.

It was a story of adventure, excitement, and everything dreams are made of. It was simply entitled *Magorium*.

Bellini wrote as small as he could so he could fit in as much of the tale as possible. However, with only a few blank pages left, the story was almost finished.

On the other hand, Molly Mahoney never finished anything.

All her life, she had acquired nothing but several beginnings, a few middles, and absolutely no ends.

Mahoney tried to finish writing a song on the piano. Unfortunately, every time she played it, she would stop at the same place. She left the piano, walked through her half-painted apartment, and out of the building. She was headed to her job at the most fabulous toy store in the city — Mr. Magorium's Wonder Emporium.

The Emporium was more than a simple toy store. It was a magical place filled with every toy imaginable. From dolls to pop-up books, bouncing balls to chemistry sets, everything seemed to come alive. More than *seemed*. For those who believed, young and old, the toys literally came to life.

As Mahoney entered, the store sprang to life. The toys appeared to wake from a good night's sleep. Windup toys whirred as Mahoney passed. Plush animals stretched and yawned. And Bellini emerged from the basement with a fresh set of children's books.

When Mahoney opened the cash register with a DING, dolls' eyes lit, hanging kites swayed, and puppets waved.

"Good morning," Mahoney told the store.

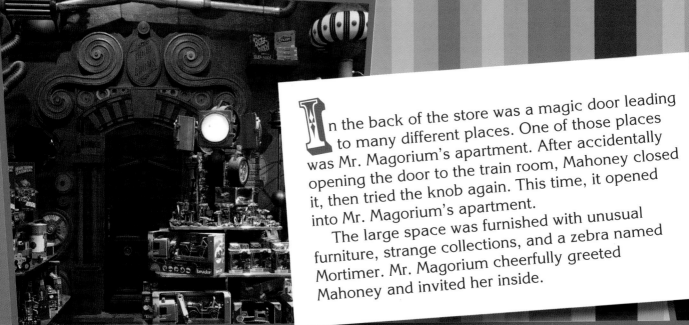

In the back of the store was a magic door leading to many different places. One of those places was Mr. Magorium's apartment. After accidentally opening the door to the train room, Mahoney closed it, then tried the knob again. This time, it opened into Mr. Magorium's apartment.

The large space was furnished with unusual furniture, strange collections, and a zebra named Mortimer. Mr. Magorium cheerfully greeted Mahoney and invited her inside.

Edward Magorium was a short, gray-haired man with kind eyes set beneath big bushy eyebrows. Although he was quite old, the man was brimming with energy and wonder. He hardly seemed like someone who could have owned the shop for 113 years.

He gave Mahoney a wooden block called a Congreve Cube.
"It looks like a big block of wood," said Mahoney.
"Now it's *your* big block of wood," said Mr. Magorium. "Unlikely adventures require unlikely tools."
"Are we going on an adventure?" asked Mahoney.
Mr. Magorium smiled. **"We're already on one."**

Mr. Magorium and Mahoney went into the store and unlocked the front doors. As usual, a steady stream of customers flowed in. Mr. Magorium watched with delight as children of all ages played with the toys in his store.

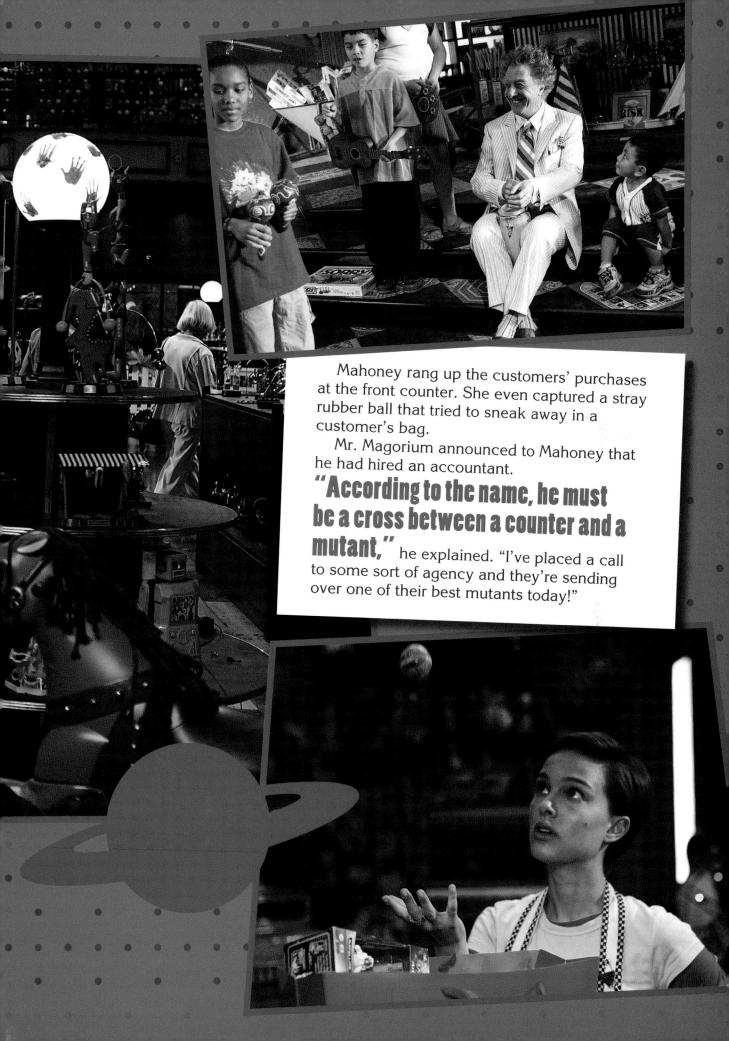

Mahoney rang up the customers' purchases at the front counter. She even captured a stray rubber ball that tried to sneak away in a customer's bag.

Mr. Magorium announced to Mahoney that he had hired an accountant.

"According to the name, he must be a cross between a counter and a mutant," he explained. "I've placed a call to some sort of agency and they're sending over one of their best mutants today!"

T

he accountant's name was Henry Weston. He was a serious man dressed in a serious suit. He strode through the store, without noticing the magical mobiles above him or the toy cars whizzing by his feet. Henry was all business.

After a short interview during which Mr. Magorium asked questions like, "Do we really need the number four?" and **"Why are there never enough hotdog buns?"** Henry got the job.

"I've owned this store for one hundred and thirteen years," Mr. Magorium told him. "Although I've been inventing toys since the mid-1770s."

Henry couldn't believe his ears. "Did you say the 1770s?"

"Yes, sir," replied Mr. Magorium. He explained that, after all these years, he wanted to know the value of the store.

"Why do you want to know this now?" asked Henry.

"Because I'm leaving," replied Mr. Magorium. He then pointed to his shoes. "I found these shoes in a tiny shop in Tuscany and fell in love with them. I bought enough to last my whole life." Mr. Magorium smiled. "These are my last pair."

ric Applebaum worked at the Emporium as well. Although he was only nine years old, Eric spent most of his time there, alone. Large groups of kids would gather to play board games or build giant puzzles, but Eric always kept to himself. He wasn't good at making friends.

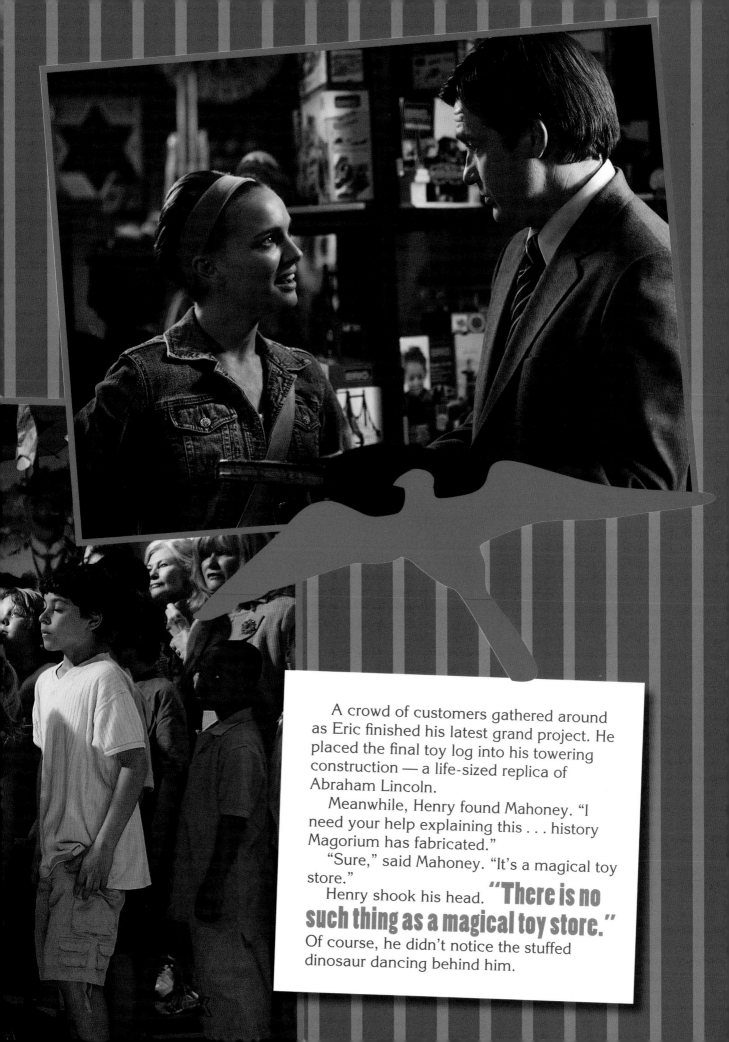

A crowd of customers gathered around as Eric finished his latest grand project. He placed the final toy log into his towering construction — a life-sized replica of Abraham Lincoln.

Meanwhile, Henry found Mahoney. "I need your help explaining this . . . history Magorium has fabricated."

"Sure," said Mahoney. "It's a magical toy store."

Henry shook his head. **"There is no such thing as a magical toy store."** Of course, he didn't notice the stuffed dinosaur dancing behind him.

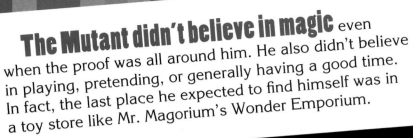

The Mutant didn't believe in magic even when the proof was all around him. He also didn't believe in playing, pretending, or generally having a good time. In fact, the last place he expected to find himself was in a toy store like Mr. Magorium's Wonder Emporium.

As Henry worked in the office, Eric watched him through the main window. Eric scribbled a message on a piece of paper. *Hi*, it read.

Henry waved, then went back to work. Eric held up another note. *Do you like checkers?*

Henry sighed and wrote his own message. *I did when I was a kid.*

Eric wrote another. *You want to play?*

Henry jotted down a reply. *I have to work.*

Eric wrote, *How about when you stop working?*

Henry held up a reply. *I never stop working.*

Eric frowned and scribbled a final message for Henry. *That's sad.*

The next day, Mr. Magorium had a surprise for Mahoney.
"I'm giving you the store," he announced.
"You're giving me the store?" asked Mahoney.
Mr. Magorium smiled. "Surprise!"

"Sir, I can't take the Emporium," she said.
"But you need it," said Mr. Magorium.
"What if I don't want it?" Mahoney asked.
Mr. Magorium frowned. "Why would you not want the Emporium?"
"Because I can't run it," she replied. "It's Mr. Magorium's Wonder Emporium. It rhymes. Not to mention the fact that you're magical and I'm not."

As Mahoney argued, a corner of the toy store lost its color. A gray splotch spread across the wall. In fact, the more she argued, the more the gray spread.

"What are you going to do if I own the store?" asked Mahoney.

"I'm leaving," said Mr. Magorium.

"Excuse me," said a young boy tugging on Mr. Magorium's sleeve. "There's something wrong, sir."

Mahoney and Mr. Magorium looked up to see the patch of gray. It had spread into the finger-painting area. All of the paints had turned gray.

"What's wrong?" asked Mahoney.

"Sadness. Confusion," Mr. Magorium replied. **"Apparently, despite my best efforts, the store is not taking my departure very well."**

The store did more than just turn gray; it had a tantrum.
The balls no longer bounced, yo-yos tangled around anyone who tried them, and model planes dive-bombed passing customers.

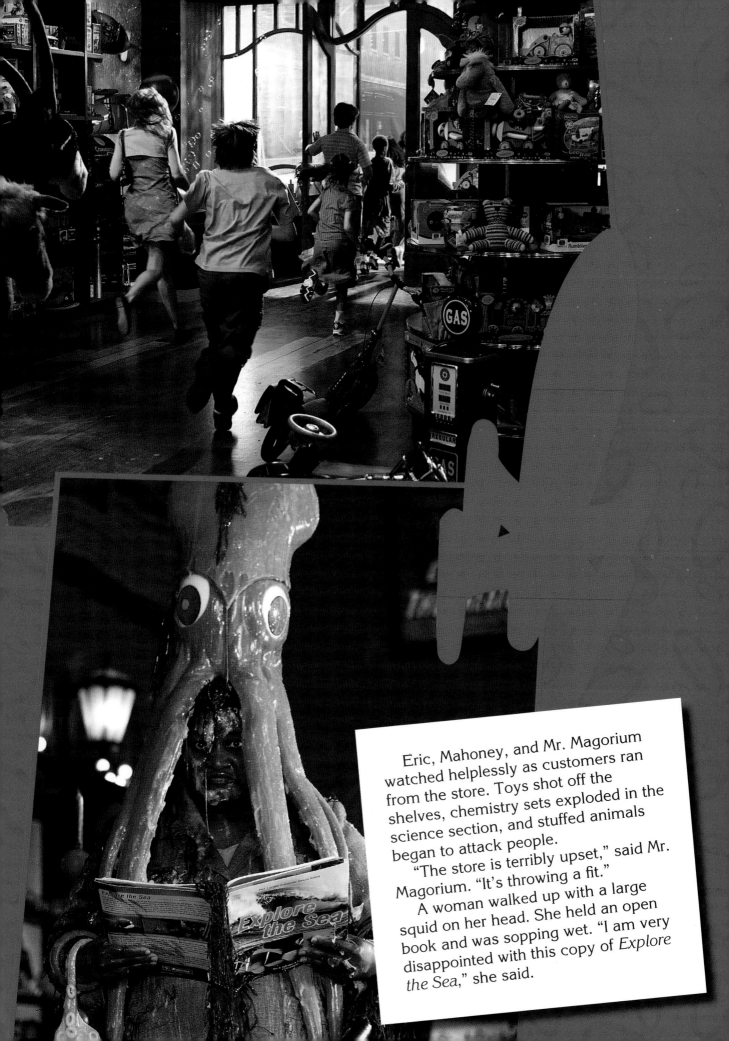

Eric, Mahoney, and Mr. Magorium watched helplessly as customers ran from the store. Toys shot off the shelves, chemistry sets exploded in the science section, and stuffed animals began to attack people.

"The store is terribly upset," said Mr. Magorium. "It's throwing a fit."

A woman walked up with a large squid on her head. She held an open book and was sopping wet. "I am very disappointed with this copy of *Explore the Sea*," she said.

Mr. Magorium closed the store and called a meeting in his apartment. "The store is stunningly upset," he announced with a bang of his toy gavel. "As indicated by its temper tantrum."

"How can a store have a temper tantrum?" asked Henry.

Mr. Magorium glanced around. "Did no one tell this Mutant that it's a magical toy store?"

"I tried," said Mahoney.

"This didn't happen until Henry showed up," said Eric.

"Me?" asked Henry.

Mr. Magorium shook his head. "Although Mr. Weston's presence has coincided with the store's dismay, it is not the cause. He's only here to draw up my will."

"Why is there a will?" asked Mahoney.

Magorium smiled. "I told you, my sweet, I'm leaving."

"Are you dying?" asked Mahoney.

Mr. Magorium laughed.

"Light bulbs die. I will depart."

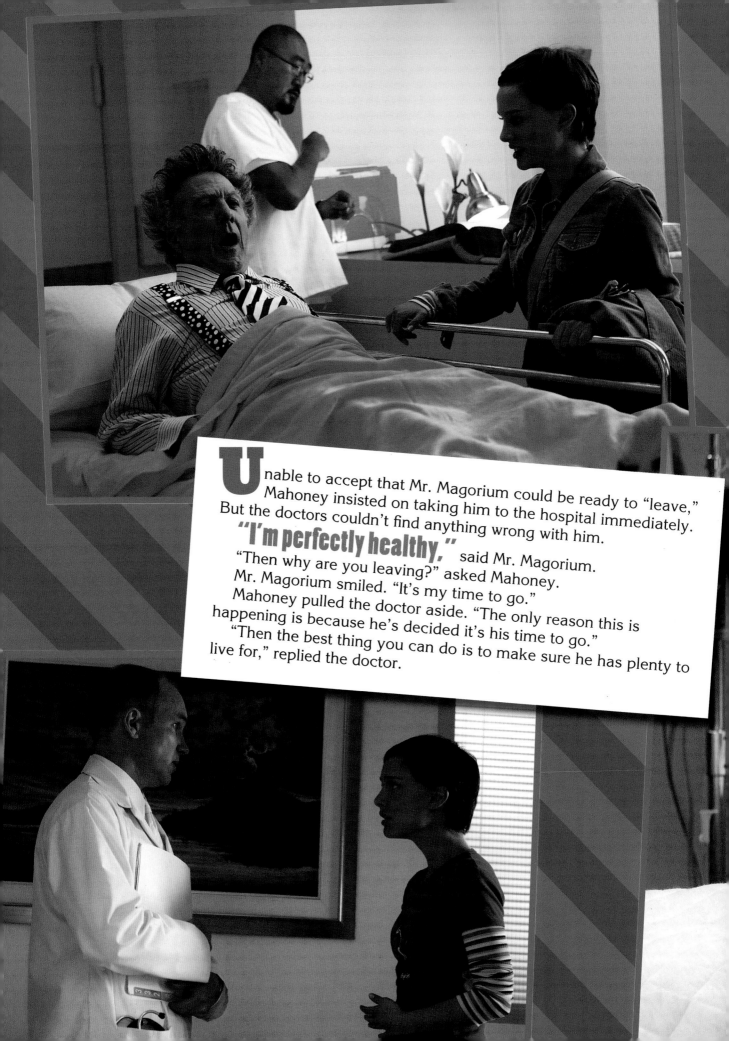

Unable to accept that Mr. Magorium could be ready to "leave," Mahoney insisted on taking him to the hospital immediately. But the doctors couldn't find anything wrong with him.

"I'm perfectly healthy," said Mr. Magorium.

"Then why are you leaving?" asked Mahoney.

Mr. Magorium smiled. "It's my time to go."

Mahoney pulled the doctor aside. "The only reason this is happening is because he's decided it's his time to go."

"Then the best thing you can do is to make sure he has plenty to live for," replied the doctor.

As Mahoney spoke with the doctor, Eric entered with a bag of goodies. One of them was a big shiny, loud horn — a euphonium. Unfortunately, Mr. Magorium was only able to play a few loud notes before the doctor took it away from him.

The next day, Mr. Magorium left the hospital with Mahoney. She had planned a special day for him, to convince him that there was plenty to live for. Instead of returning to the Emporium, she took him to a mattress store.

"Follow me," she instructed. "Do as I do and then run out the door."

"All right," agreed Mr. Magorium.

Mahoney glanced around. "I'm a little nervous about this."

"Why?" asked Mr. Magorium.

"Because it's mischievous and childish," she replied.

Mr. Magorium smiled. "I can hardly wait."

Suddenly, Mahoney ran and jumped onto one of the mattresses. She bounded high into the air and leaped to the mattress beside it. Mr. Magorium followed her as she bounded onto mattress after mattress. The two laughed as they hopped around the store. When they came to the last one, they jumped onto the floor and ran out the door before the store manager could catch them.

mahoney took Mr. Magorium for some ice cream and then for another special surprise. She bought a roll of bubble wrap and spread it on the sidewalk.

"Now what?" asked Mr. Magorium.
"DANCE!" instructed Mahoney.

Mr. Magorium leaped onto the bubble wrap and began to dance. Tiny plastic bubbles popped under his feet with each step. Mahoney soon joined him and they danced together.

"This is terribly sweet of you, my dear," said Mr. Magorium.

"I wanted you to see all the little things you'll miss if you leave," she told him.

Mr. Magorium frowned. "And I thought you were giving me the best last day of anyone who ever lived."

"This can't be your last day, sir," said Mahoney.

Mr. Magorium smiled. "Ah, but it is." He gave her a hug. "And thanks to you, it looks to be a remarkable one."

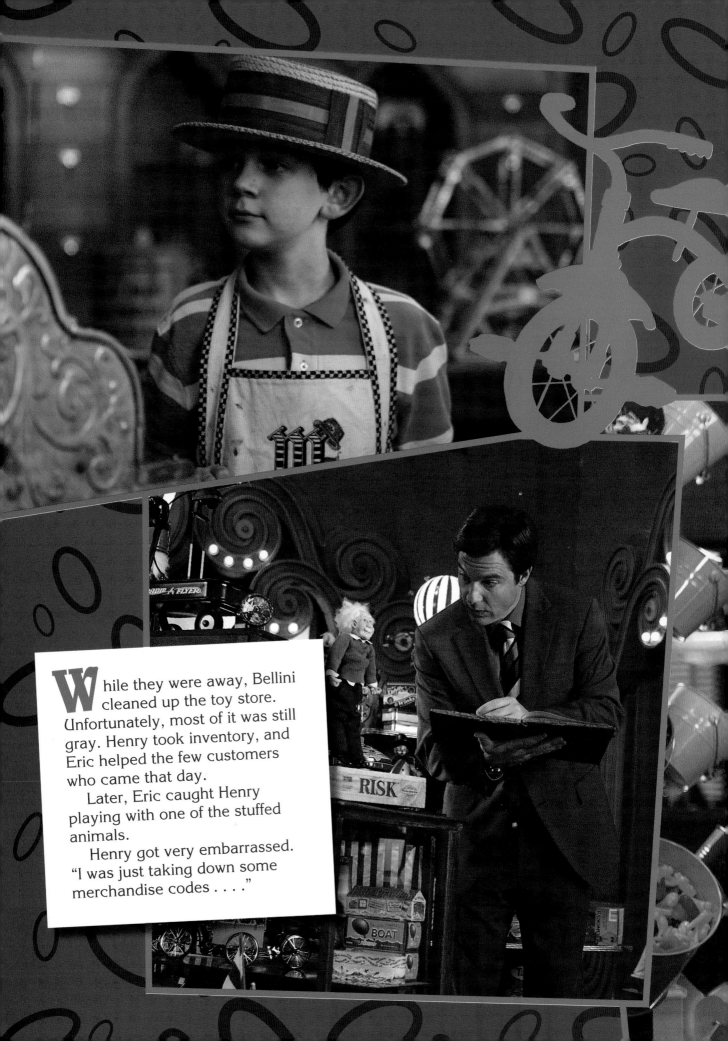

While they were away, Bellini cleaned up the toy store. Unfortunately, most of it was still gray. Henry took inventory, and Eric helped the few customers who came that day.

Later, Eric caught Henry playing with one of the stuffed animals.

Henry got very embarrassed. "I was just taking down some merchandise codes . . . ."

"You mean, pretending?" asked Eric.

"It's not pretending," said Henry. "I was just doing this to keep my mind active while there wasn't much else to think about."

"Yeah," said Eric. "That's called pretending."

Eric smiled. **"It's okay, Mutant.** You can stay out here and play with the toys. I won't tell anyone."

After they closed the store for the day, Eric asked Henry if he wanted to see his hat collection. Henry had never heard of anyone who collected hats.

"Oh my," said Henry when he saw the wall full of hats.

"You want to try one on?" asked Eric.

"No, that's all right," said Henry.

Eric smiled. "I think we both know you want to try on a hat."

Soon Henry had not only tried on a hat, he was pretending again. Eric wore a crown, while Henry wore a court jester's hat. Eric pretended to order him to brush the dragon's teeth with a giant toothbrush.

Molly Mahoney was very sad when she brought Mr. Magorium back to the store. She knew this was the last time she would see him.

"I love you," she said.

"I love you, too," he replied.

A tear rolled down her cheek. "Is there anything I can do?"

"Find your life," he replied. Then he gave her a big hug. "I'm so proud of you."

Mahoney smiled. "I haven't done anything yet."

"I know," said Mr. Magorium. "But you will."

Mahoney left. Mr. Magorium was alone in his store. It looked like a dark, dreary, very ordinary store. It didn't seem magical at all.

"I had hoped you would have improved by now," he told the store. **"You must hold on. She will find it.** She will give you all that you need." He sat down on a small stool and looked around. "You have been my greatest achievement, my shining glory." Mr. Magorium looked at his store one last time. "I hate to leave you but I cannot stay. Good-bye."

M ahoney and Eric stood in the cemetery and paid their respects. Mr. Magorium had a simple gravestone that read, *"Toy Impresario, Wonder Aficionado, Avid Shoe-Wearer."*

As Mahoney and Eric left, they passed a long line of people waiting to pay their respects as well. There were friends, customers, and even Mortimer the zebra. The line stretched as far as the eye could see.

The next day, Eric found the toy store closed.

The windows were dark. The doors were locked. And there was a *For Sale* sign in the window.

FOR SALE

PUSH

Eric went looking for Mahoney. He found her in a hotel lobby. She was wearing a fancy dress and playing piano for the guests. Although the music sounded cheerful, Mahoney's face was not.

Eric marched up to her. "What are you doing?"

Mahoney stopped playing and hung her head. "I have to make money."

"Then run the store," he said.

"I would love to run the store," she said with a sigh. "But I can't. I'm not Mr. Magorium, and I can't be a kid anymore."

"I know," Eric agreed. "You have to start the rest of your life."

"Exactly," Mahoney muttered.

Eric clenched his fists. **"But your life is in that store!"**

That night, Mahoney sat in the store and stared at Mr. Magorium's Congreve Cube. It was supposed to help her, but she didn't know how to use it.

Henry arrived and told her that someone had offered to buy the store. But, he didn't think she should sell.

"You don't even believe in this store, Mutant," said Mahoney.

Henry smiled. "But I believe in you."

"I'm not much to believe in." She set the cube down. "Mr. Magorium could make the wildest, most improbable, most ludicrous thing happen with a flick of the wrist. I can't even finish what I start."

Henry shook his head. "Do you honestly believe that this store was magic?"

Mahoney wiped a tear from her eye. **"Absolutely. I believe it with my entire heart."**

Behind her, the Congreve Cube flipped onto one side. Henry's eyes widened. In fact, the more Mahoney insisted that the store was magical, the more the cube rumbled and jerked.

Wondering what Henry was staring at, Mahoney turned and saw the cube flipping from side to side. She smiled and ran over to the animated block of wood. "You can do better than that," she said. "Move!"

The cube spun down the counter and took to the air. As it zipped around the store, Henry promptly passed out.

Molly Mahoney realized what was wrong with the store. It just wanted someone to believe in it. And even though many people did believe, the store needed someone who didn't believe in anything at all — Henry!

The next morning, Mahoney was there when Henry woke. "I'm ready to sell the store," she announced.

Henry stumbled to his feet. "You can't!"

"Why can't I?" she asked with a smirk.

"Because it's magic!" he shouted.

Suddenly, a shelf full of toys came to life. Their color returned as they began to move by themselves.

Mahoney rolled her eyes. "What makes you believe that?"

"The cube," he replied. "It flew around the store!"

The store's dull grayness shrank away as more sparkling color appeared.

Kites began to sway, cars began to roll, and dolls began to speak.

Suddenly, Mahoney realized that it was more than Henry believing. Mr. Magorium had really wanted *her* to believe in herself. A chill shot down her spine. "Wait a minute," she said. "*I'm* the block of wood."

Henry smiled. "And apparently a block of wood can do anything."

Mahoney moved her fingers, and a toy piano played the song she had been writing. As she moved around the store, more toys joined in. They glowed with bright color and soon her tune played from everything in the store.

The front doors burst open and Eric and several customers poured inside. Everyone laughed as the store came to life. Mahoney and Henry danced with joy. In the stuffed animal section, all the animals gave them a great big hug.

Molly Mahoney finally finished her song. It filled the Emporium with life and magic once more.

She found the sparkle Mr. Magorium had always seen in her. Now, she walked around the store helping people make their wildest dreams come true.

Henry began working in the store as well. He loved finding just the right toy for each customer. And he was always excited to point out some of his favorites.

Eric found he could make friends now. He had no trouble inviting them to join in on his amazing toy constructions.

Bellini the bookmaker smiled as he delivered a fresh batch of children's books from the basement. Once his task was complete, he returned to work on a very important book.

He opened a fresh volume and began writing: Chapter One.

This is the story of Molly Mahoney. This is a story of tremendous adventure, enormous love, unexpected trials, and expected tribulations. This story takes place in a familiar world, but someplace she never would have imagined. It is a story told simply. It is an amazing tale of an amazing woman who lived an amazing life.

And it begins right now . . .